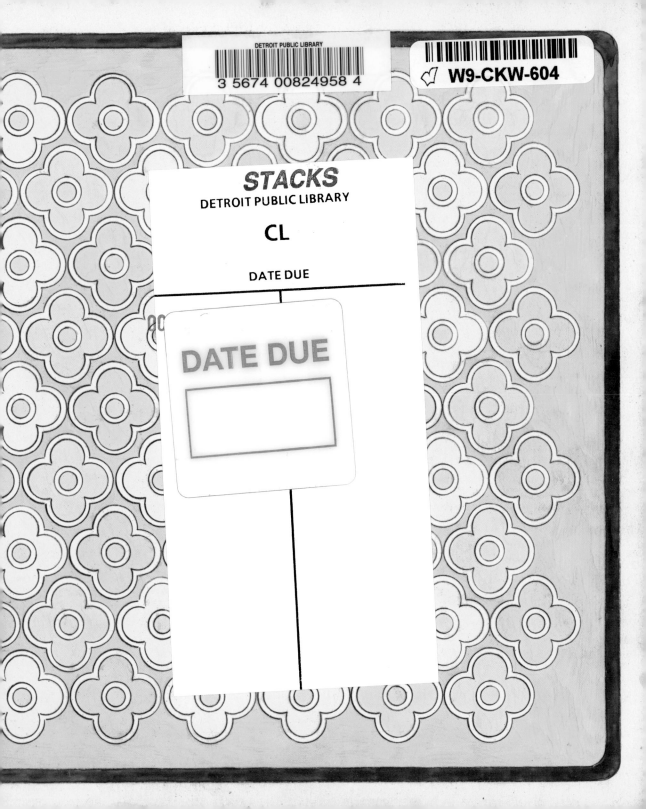

ALMOST TWINS

ALMOST
TWINS

**Story and Pictures
by
Dale Payson**

Prentice-Hall Inc. Englewood Cliffs, N.J.

10 9 8 7 6 5 4 3 2 1

Copyright © 1974 by Dale Payson

Printed in the United States of America •J

Prentice-Hall International, Inc., London
Prentice-Hall of Australia, Pty. Ltd., North Sydney
Prentice-Hall of Canada, Ltd., Toronto
Prentice-Hall of India Private Ltd., New Delhi
Prentice-Hall of Japan, Inc., Tokyo

Library of Congress Cataloging in Publication
Data

Payson, Dale.
    Almost twins.

    SUMMARY: Everyone says Annabelle and
Nellie are almost twins, but Annabelle, strug-
gling to measure up to her older sister's accom-
plishments, knows different.
    [1. Brothers and sisters—Fiction] I. Title.
PZ7.P299Al   [E]   74-5044
ISBN 0-13-022780-3

In the same village, on the same road, in the same house lived two sisters, Nellie and Annabelle. Even though Nellie was almost a year older than Annabelle, they looked alike and they went to the same school, and they both loved rhubarb pie. Everyone thought they were almost twins.

Even Great Aunt Bessie. She always made sure their dresses matched, and their hats matched, and their aprons matched and when Nellie had bows in her hair, so did Annabelle.

Aunt Bessie loved them both very much and never hugged one without hugging the other.

In the winter when Aunt Bessie took
Nellie and Annabelle ice skating, she
always said they were both good skaters
. . . but Annabelle thought that Nellie
could really skate a little bit better.

Aunt Bessie always said they both did very neat embroidery. But Annabelle thought that Nellie's stitches were really a little bit neater.

Aunt Bessie said that they were both good cooks but Annabelle thought that Nellie's cake was really a little bit higher.

When they worked in their gardens, Aunt Bessie said they were both good gardeners but when summer came Annabelle thought that Nellie's garden was really a little bit brighter.

Whatever Nellie did, Annabelle did. They even celebrated their birthdays at the same party. As Nellie opened her biggest present, all the boys and girls crowded around her.

Annabelle picked out the smallest present and slowly unwrapped it.

Inside, Annabelle found a little paint set. She closed her eyes and saw the beautiful pictures she would paint. She couldn't wait to start.

When the party was over and everyone had gone home, Annabelle said to Nellie, "Let's paint."

Aunt Bessie said they both painted very nice pictures, but this time Annabelle thought that her picture was just as nice as Nellie's.

The following day, Annabelle said to
Nellie, "Let's paint." But Nellie said, "No,
I'd rather play dolls." So they did.

The next time Annabelle said to Nellie, "Let's paint," Nellie said, "No, I'd rather play outside." So they did.

Annabelle waited a whole week before she said to Nellie again "Let's paint." Nellie said, "Painting is so dumb, *I'd* rather jump rope." So they did.

The last time Annabelle said to Nellie, "Let's paint," Nellie said, "No, I'm busy."

"Too busy to paint?" asked Annabelle.

"I'm making a surprise for Aunt Bessie's birthday," said Nellie, "and you can't help."

Annabelle didn't know what to do. No cake she could bake would be as good as Nellie's. No sampler she could sew would be as neat as Nellie's. And all the flowers in her garden wouldn't make a bouquet as pretty as Nellie's.

Annabelle thought and thought and finally decided to make a surprise for Aunt Bessie that would surprise Nellie too.

She could hardly wait for dinner to be over so that she could give Aunt Bessie her present.

After dinner, Nellie brought in the birthday cake she had made all by herself. Aunt Bessie said it was the most beautiful birthday cake she had ever had.

When Annabelle saw how beautiful Nellie's cake was, she didn't want to give Aunt Bessie her present.

Nellie said to Annabelle, "What do you have for Aunt Bessie?"

Annabelle gave Aunt Bessie her present. Aunt Bessie didn't say a word, but she smiled as she showed it to Nellie.

**Aunt Bessie said this was the best birth-
day she'd ever had. "And," she whispered
to Annabelle, "your present is just as nice
as Nellie's."**

This time Annabelle knew it was true.

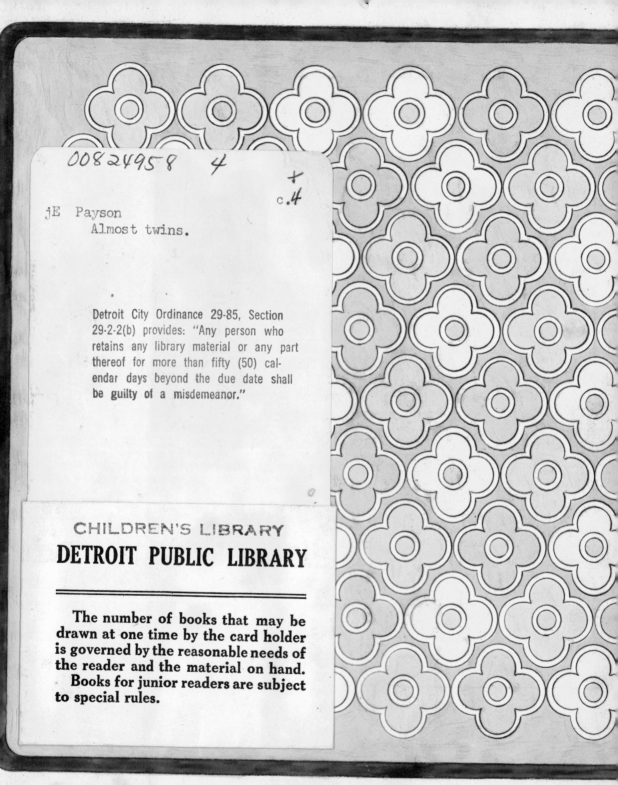